Bird and Bear

by Ann James

little bee books

"Welcome to the world, baby Hanno!" says Bird.
"All aboard!!" says Bear.

A peanut is for sharing

little bee books
An imprint of Bonnier Publishing Group
853 Broadway, New York, New York 10003
Text and illustration copyright © 2013 by Ann James.
First published in Australia by The Five Mile Press. This little bee books edition, 2015.
All rights reserved, including the right of reproduction in whole or in part in any form.
LITTLE BEE BOOKS is a trademark of Bonnier Publishing Group, and associated
colophon is a trademark of Bonnier Publishing Group.
Manufactured in China 0115 LEO
First Edition 2 4 6 8 10 9 7 5 3 1
Library of Congress Control Number: 2014943760
ISBN 978-1-4998-0037-1

www.littlebeebooks.com
www.bonnierpublishing.com

Today is Bear's birthday.

Tap! Tap! Tap!
"Wake up, Bear!"

"Good morning, Bird," says Bear.
"Would you like some breakfast?"

"Happy bearthday, Bear!" Bird says. "Here's a present.
It's a peanut. It has two delicious nuts inside."

"How thoughtful," says Bear. "Thanks, Bird.
What should we do today?"

"Get dressed, Bear!"
says Bird.

"Quick, Bear! Put your boots on!"

"Who's that?" asks Bird.

"That's my friend, the other bear," says Bear.

"He looks just like you," Bird says.

"Is it a sunny day or a rainy day, Bear?"
asks Bird.

"It's a sunny day," says Bear.
"Let's have a picnic."

"A birthday picnic!" says Bird,
"and a red bucket might come in handy."

"All aboard!" calls Bear.

"Off we go!" calls Bird.

Out the gate they walk,

down the street ...

and **across** the crosswalk.

Through the park they go,

over the sand ...

up the steps ...

. . . to the pier.
   "We're here!" says Bear.

"Look!" says Bird. "The other bear is here, too."

"So he is," says Bear. "And look!
There's another bird who looks just like you!"

"How about that?" says Bird.

"My tummy's rumbling," says Bear.
"It must be picnic time."

"Uh-oh!" calls Bird.
"The other bear is gone."

"Maybe he's over here," says Bear.

"Here they both are!" says Bird.

"That's good," says Bear as
he gets the picnic ready.

"One for me ...."

"and one for you ..."

"... and one for the
other bear," says Bear.

"And some crumbs for the
other bird," says Bird.

Suddenly the water ripples.

"Ohhhh!"

"So, it's not a real bear," says Bear.

"And it's not a real bird," says Bird.

Then Bear smiles.

"Let's play a bearthday game," he says.

"And let's take the red bucket," says Bird.

"Hello, other bear.
Hello, other bird," says Bear.

"Goodbye, other bear.
Goodbye, other bird!"

"Time to go," says Bear.
"All aboard!"

"Off we go again!" calls Bird.

Along the pier they walk.
"I liked having a friend who
was just like me," says Bear.

Down
the
steps.

" Me too," says Bird.

And **over** the sand.

"But," says Bear, "it's good to have a
friend who is different."

"Yes, it is," says Bird.

Through the park they go.

"It's nice to have someone to talk to," says Bird.

Across the crosswalk.
"Very nice," says Bear.

And **down** the street.
"Do you have a birdday, Bird?"
asks Bear.

"I have a hatchday," says Bird,
"and it's coming up soon."

They stop at Bear's gate.

"We could do something special for your hatchday, Bird," says Bear.

"Let's!" says Bird.

"See you tomorrow, Bird!"

"See you tomorrow, Bear!"